Weekly Reader Children's Book Club presents

Eugene
the Brave

by Ellen Conford
Illustrated by John Larrecq

LITTLE, BROWN AND COMPANY

Boston   Toronto

Other Books About the Possum Family

Impossible Possum
Illustrated by Rosemary Wells
Just the Thing for Geraldine
Illustrated by John Larrecq

This book is a presentation of Weekly
Reader Children's Book Club.
Weekly Reader Children's Book Club
offers book clubs for children from
preschool to young adulthood. All
quality hardcover books are selected
by a distinguished Weekly Reader
Selection Board.

For further information write to:
Weekly Reader Children's Book Club
1250 Fairwood Ave.
Columbus, Ohio 43216

Library of Congress Cataloging in Publication Data

Conford, Ellen.
    Eugene the brave.

    SUMMARY: Eugene, a possum, hopes to escape his
fear of the dark by sleeping all night. His sister
Geraldine tries to help.
    [1. Fear — Fiction. 2. Night — Fiction.
3. Opossums — Fiction] I. Larrecq, John M.
II. Title.
PZ7.C7593Eu   [E]   77-24241
ISBN 0-316-15292-7

*Published simultaneously in Canada
by Little, Brown & Company (Canada) Limited*

PRINTED IN THE UNITED STATES OF AMERICA

ALL OF A SUDDEN, for no reason at all,
Eugene was afraid of the dark.

"But Eugene," said his mother, "you've never been afraid of the dark before."

"That may be true," said Eugene, "but I'm afraid now."

"There's nothing to be afraid of," said his brother Randolph. "The dark is just when the sun goes down. And sometimes there's a moon, so it's not very dark at all."

"And sometimes there isn't," said his sister Geraldine, "and it's pitch-black." She tried to stand on her head.

"But even when there isn't a moon, the stars are out," said Randolph.

"Except if it's raining," said Geraldine. "Or cloudy. Then it's pitch-black." She lost her balance and nearly fell out of the tree. "Whoops," she said, grabbing the branch just in time.

"Eugene," said his father, "we sleep during the day and stay up during the night. How will you learn to look for food and take care of a family of your own if you're afraid of the dark?"

"I don't know," said Eugene. "That might be a problem."

"It certainly will be a problem," agreed his mother.

"I'm standing on my head!" yelled Geraldine. "Look, everybody! See me standing on my head?"

"I can hardly see you at all, Geraldine," said Eugene. He shivered. "It's getting dark, isn't it? The sun isn't out anymore."

"That's right," said his father. "It's time for us to get food."

"Are you going to be big and brave and come with us?" Eugene's mother asked hopefully.

"I'd rather be little and weak and have you stay home with me," he said.

"But we can't stay home. We have to get food. You want to eat, don't you?" asked his father.

"I'm really not very hungry," said Eugene.

"I'm starved," said Geraldine. She tossed a blackberry in the air and caught it in her mouth.

"Geraldine and I can stay home with
Eugene," Randolph suggested. "That way
you can get the food and we can keep him
company."

"All right," sighed his father, "but something will have to be done about this."

Their mother and father went off to find
food, and Eugene, Randolph, and Geraldine
stayed on the branch of their tree.

"It's awfully dark now, isn't it?" asked
Eugene, in a squeaky voice.

"There's a star," Randolph pointed. "See?"

"It's a very little star," Geraldine said.
"Not a bright star at all." She juggled some
acorns as she hung by her tail from the
branch.

Suddenly there was a *plip!* beneath the tree.

"What was that?" cried Eugene.

"I dropped an acorn," said Geraldine. "I'll get it." She ran down the tree.

There was a rustling, scuffling sound under the branch.

"What is that?" Eugene grabbed Randolph.

"That's me looking for the acorn," Geraldine called. "Don't worry, I found it." She ran back up the tree and sat down next to Eugene. She began to juggle again.

Plip. Plip. Plop.

Eugene jumped.

"I don't know what's the matter with me today," sighed Geraldine. "I dropped three more of them."

"Maybe you'd better not juggle anymore," said Randolph. "You're making Eugene nervous."

"Oh. All right. I wasn't doing very well anyway."

"It's getting darker and darker," Eugene whispered. "And I'm getting scareder and scareder."

"There isn't anything to be afraid of," Randolph assured him.

"Certainly not," agreed Geraldine. "We're perfectly safe here. Really, Eugene, you're acting like a big baby. You'd think the woods were full of grizzly bears and rattlesnakes and big, hairy spiders."

Eugene gave a little shriek.

"And you're way up here in the tree," Geraldine went on, "so nothing could sneak up behind you. Except maybe a vampire bat," she added.

"Eee!" Eugene squealed in terror. He grabbed Randolph around the middle, clutching him tightly.

At the sound of Eugene's scream, their mother and father came running.

"What's the matter?" asked their father.

"Are you all right?" asked their mother. She ran up the tree. Eugene let go of Randolph and clung to her, trembling.

"Don't go away," pleaded Eugene. "It's too scary without you here."

"All right, all right," she said gently, patting Eugene. "I'll stay with you for now. Maybe tomorrow night you will feel braver."

"Of course he will," said his father.

"And maybe there will be a nice, bright moon out tomorrow," said Randolph.

Geraldine hung upside down and swayed gently back and forth by her tail.

"I think it might rain," she said.

The next evening after the sun went down, their father said, "Come along, Eugene. We're going to look for food now."

"I'm too tired," said Eugene. He yawned. "I didn't sleep a wink all day."

"But why not?" asked his mother. "We always sleep in the daytime."

"I know, but I'm going to sleep at night and stay up during the day from now on. That way I won't have to be awake in the scary time."

"I don't think that's a very sensible idea," said his father.

"I don't think that will work out at all," said his mother.

"I think that's the silliest thing I ever heard," said Geraldine.

"Are you going to stay here all by yourself?" asked Randolph.

"No!" said Eugene. "Couldn't you stay with me until I fall asleep? I'm so tired I'm sure I'll be asleep in no time."

His father sighed. "I don't know why you have to do things backwards, Eugene."

"This just isn't natural," his mother said.

"Maybe he'll grow out of it," Randolph suggested.

Geraldine balanced a chestnut on her nose.

Eugene curled his tail around the branch of the tree and hung upside down. He closed his eyes.

Suddenly his eyes flew open and he sat up on the branch.

His father and mother and Randolph and Geraldine were sitting in a row, looking at him.

"I feel like someone's watching me!" he cried.

"We're *all* watching you," said Geraldine. "We're waiting for you to fall asleep."

"Well, I can't fall asleep with you staring at me that way," said Eugene. "You're making me very nervous."

The possums turned around so their backs were to Eugene.

"Is that better?" asked Randolph.

"Much better," said Eugene. "Thank you." He curled his tail around the tree branch and hung upside down again. He closed his eyes. He was really very, very sleepy. He was so sleepy that he was soon sound asleep.

When he woke up it was very dark and there was no one on the branch but him.

Suddenly he heard a strange noise. Something was scampering up the tree, right toward his branch! Eugene was more frightened than he had ever been before. He couldn't move; he couldn't make a sound. He just held his breath and closed his eyes tightly, afraid even to look at what was coming up the tree toward him.

"Are you awake, Eugene?"

"Geraldine!" Eugene gasped and opened his eyes. "Why didn't you say something? Why did you sneak up on me like that?"

"I didn't mean to sneak up on you," she said. "I was being quiet because I thought you were still asleep."

"Is everyone else gone?" asked Eugene.

"Yes. I thought you might want someone to be here if you woke up, so I decided to stay. Why don't you try and go back to sleep?"

"You scared me so much I don't think I'm sleepy anymore."

"Maybe it would help if I sang you a lullaby."

"I don't know," Eugene said doubtfully. "Do you know any nice lullabies?"

"I'll make one up," said Geraldine. She began to sing, in her softest, sweetest voice:

There are no monsters here,
There's nothing you should fear,
No giant armadillo,
Is hiding in the willow,
No dragon breathing smoke,
Will make you cough and choke,
No vampire bat with glowing eyes,
Is going to take you by surprise,
No ghost in white, or goblin green,
Is whispering, "Eugene…Eugene…"

Eugene's eyes opened wide.

"Geraldine?" he squeaked. "Could you stop singing now?"

"Oh," said Geraldine, sounding disappointed. "I was just getting started. Did I make you nice and sleepy?"

"Not really," said Eugene. "In fact, I'm wider awake than ever."

From then on, Eugene stayed home with Randolph or Geraldine while their parents went to look for food. His mother and father kept reminding him that he could not go on forever sleeping at night and staying up during the day, but Eugene kept being afraid.

One evening, just as the sun was going down, Geraldine said, "I've been thinking, Eugene, and I have a way to cure you of being afraid."

"How?" asked Eugene.

"I'm going to try to scare you. We'll start out with something just a little scary, and work up to something big."

"How will that cure me?" asked Eugene.

"Because you'll get *used* to being scared and it won't bother you so much."

"I don't know—" said Eugene.

"BOO!" shouted Geraldine, jumping toward him.

Eugene laughed. "Boo yourself," he said. "That wasn't scary at all."

"You're braver than I thought," said Geraldine. "I'll have to try something scarier." She turned her back to him and began to wail, "Ooo—eee—oooh."

"What *is* that?" their mother called.

"That's just Geraldine," Eugene called back. "She's trying to scare me. But she's not doing very well."

"She scared *me*," his mother replied.

Geraldine began to shake the branch they were sitting on. She made it shake very gently at first, then harder and harder, until Eugene had to hang on tightly to keep from being thrown off.

"What is shaking the tree?" Randolph called. "What's happening?"

"It's just Geraldine," said Eugene. "She's trying to scare me."

"It must be an earthquake," Geraldine said, pretending to be frightened. "Eugene, it's an earthquake!"

"I know it's you, Geraldine," he said. "You're not scaring me at all."

The branch stopped shaking.

"Hmmm," muttered Geraldine. "You're *much* braver than I thought. I'm going to have to do something a lot scarier before I can frighten you."

She ran down the tree and Eugene saw her scamper behind a bush. The leaves of the bush began to rustle.

"Eu-gee-eene," came a mysterious voice. "Eu-gee-eene, I seeeee youuu . . ."

"I see *you* behind that bush, Geraldine."

"I'm not Geraldine," said the voice. "I'm a ghost. If you don't believe me, come and find out for your-se-elf."

"I'm coming," said Eugene. He ran down the tree and toward the bush. But Geraldine had climbed halfway up another tree while he was coming down.

"I really *am* a ghost and you can't seeee meee," said the spooky voice.

"I can see you," said Eugene, "when you're not hiding."

"Ooo-eee-oooh," wailed Geraldine. She ran down the tree and crawled inside a hollow log. Eugene ran after her as she scrambled out the other end of the log.

Making her ghostly noises, Geraldine ran
from bush to bush, from tree trunk to tree
trunk, hiding in all the good places there
were to hide in the forest. Eugene followed
her everywhere. He didn't even notice that
the sun had set and it was nighttime.

Suddenly there was a loud crash and a
scream. Eugene stopped dead in his tracks.
He whirled around, trying to see where the
noise had come from.

But he could hardly see anything, because
it was very dark.

"Help!" came Geraldine's voice. "Eugene, help me!"

"G-G-Geraldine?" stammered Eugene. "Are you still t-t-trying to scare me?"

"No! Listen to me! I'm stuck! Come and help me! There might be snakes in here!"

"S-s-snakes?" Eugene's teeth chattered. "In *where*?"

"In this hole! Come and get me *out*! I'm trapped! Hurry up, Eugene!"

"But where are you?" he asked. "I don't see you."

"Of course you don't see me!" screamed Geraldine. "I'm in a *big hole!*"

"Well, keep screaming, Geraldine," said Eugene, trying to sound brave, "and I'll follow your voice."

"Be careful!" warned Geraldine. "Don't you fall in too."

"I'll be careful," said Eugene nervously. "Just keep talking."

"Just keep looking!" yelled Geraldine. "There may be poisonous spiders in here too for all I know!"

"Oh, I d-d-don't think there are any p-p-poisonous spiders around here," said Eugene.

He followed the sound of Geraldine's voice, looking over the ground carefully as he walked.

"Here, here I am!" called Geraldine. "Over this way."

Eugene found Geraldine in a deep hole near a raspberry bush. There were twigs and branches and leaves all around her.

"Why didn't you just climb out?" asked Eugene, looking down into the hole.

"Because I think I hurt myself when I fell," said Geraldine. "I don't know if I can walk."

"All right, be very calm," said Eugene. "I'll get a long stick and pull you out."

He found a branch nearby and leaned over the hole. He held the branch out for Geraldine to grab.

"Wrap your tail around it and hang on," he said.

Geraldine wrapped her tail around the branch. Eugene grunted and panted and strained and finally lifted the branch up out of the hole.

"There!" he gasped. Geraldine unwound her tail from the branch and sat down next to him.

"Do you think you can walk?" he asked.

"I'll try," said Geraldine weakly. "I'm not sure."

She circled around Eugene a few times, walking very lightly.

"I think I can."

"We'd better go home, then," said Eugene. "It's very dark."

"It's pitch-black," agreed Geraldine. She limped along beside her brother as they walked back to their tree.

"Were there really snakes in there?" asked Eugene.

"You never know," said Geraldine.

"I'm sure there weren't any poisonous spiders," he said.

"You can't be too sure of these things," said Geraldine. "But I don't know why *you* should worry about snakes and spiders," she added. "You of all creatures."

"What do you mean?"

"Well, you *practically* saved my life," said Geraldine. "You're *practically* a hero. And heroes are so brave they aren't afraid of anything."

"I did? I am? They aren't?" Eugene babbled excitedly.

"In fact, you couldn't possibly be afraid of the dark, because anyone who *was* couldn't have done the daring rescue you just did. It *is* pitch-black out, you know."

Geraldine was hardly limping at all now, but Eugene was so thrilled at the thought of being a hero he didn't notice.

"I had no idea I was that brave," he said proudly.

When they got back to the tree, their mother and father and Randolph were waiting for them.

"Where have you been?" their mother cried. "We were worried about you."

"I saved Geraldine's life!" shouted Eugene. "I wasn't one bit afraid, and I saved her life! *In the dark!*"

"You did?" his father exclaimed. "What happened? Are you all right, Geraldine?"

"Of course I'm all right. Eugene rescued me." And Geraldine told them what had happened.

"Isn't that amazing?" said his father.

"How brave you are," said Randolph.

"My hero!" said his mother, dabbing at a tear.

Geraldine didn't say anything.

She was too busy trying to stand on her head.